KRAMPUS

CREATURE OF THE YULETIDE

CONTENTS

CHAPTER

1

On the night of December 5th, the moon's light in the sky withered away as eerie darkness blanketed the land. A grandfather and his grandchild were gathering firewood in the woods near their home atop a hill. Shivering, the child witnessed the frosty breath leaving his lips for the first time. The rustling of the leaves in the trees quieted as the woods grew silent, and the wind came to a stop. Noticing the child trembling due to the sudden drop in temperature, the old man draped his jacket around him. He then told him to return to the house and warm up by the fireplace. While holding a small bundle of firewood, the child hurried along on his tiny legs. As he marched through the woods, the sound of twigs snapping and leaves crunching under his fluffy duck boots could be heard. Reaching the edge of the woods, his house came into sight, and his step had more of a skip to it as he made his way to the door. Running to the doorstep, he gently placed the tiny bundle of firewood into a basket and plopped down on the porch to take off his boots before going inside. The child looked up at the woods in the distance and saw two peering white eyes illuminating the dark. He could see a silhouette standing in the woods with its hand raised and long fingers with claws waving at him. The child smiled and waved back enthusiastically.

Once his boots were off, the child stood up and hurried inside, closing the door behind him. When he entered the kitchen, he turned on the electric kettle to heat up some water. He then grabbed a packet of instant hot chocolate mix and an opened bag of marshmallows from the pantry. The pitter-patter of his little feet echoed through the kitchen as he moved around, excited to drink his hot chocolate in front of the fire. The loud click of the kettle alerted his anxious body to run over to it and carefully pour the hot water into his gingerbread-themed cup. The child then topped the steamy beverage off with marshmallows. As he reached his stubby little hands into the bag again, the door swung open and heavy stomps on the wooden porch diverted his attention. The old man came inside, dusting snow off of himself as he called out to his grandson. Hearing his little footsteps in the kitchen, the old man entered and found him with his hand in the bag of marshmallows. Smiling, he patted his grandson on the head before opening the fridge and taking out a can of whipped cream and a stick of chocolate to layer on top of his creamy beverage.

Lifting his grandson in his arms, he happily took him to the fireplace. Setting him down on a stool near the fireplace, the old man walked over to the sofa and sat down to watch his grandson. Taking out his tablet, he played Christmas carols. This was his first Christmas with his grandchild, so he had brought him up to his vacation home to experience his first white Christmas. The old man soon got up and went into the kitchen to make something to drink. As he poured some hot water from the kettle, he paused for a moment when he saw the water rippling and dancing slightly in his cup. A dark shadow moved outside the window, causing the plates and cups in the kitchen sink to rattle. The old man walked to the window and peered outside into the dark night; the wooden floor of the porch creaked as several footsteps came up the steps.

"Dad, it's us," someone outside called out.

The old man opened the door for his daughter and her husband, accompanied by several of his other children coming off an RV. The house was soon filled with music and laughter. They baked cookies, made eggnog, and even unboxed holiday decorations to spruce up the house. Hanging wreaths and Christmas lights all over the house, the old man and his children spent the night decorating. In the midst of all this, he always ensured his grandchild had snacks and something to drink while he danced and played by himself near the fireplace.

Having finished decorating, everyone got comfortable around the fireplace. Wrapped in blankets with cups in hand, they shared fond Christmas memories, eventually falling asleep into the early hours of the new day. The child yawned and stretched out on his grandfather's lap. Looking over at the fireplace, he noticed it was about to go out. Rubbing his eyes, he hopped off his grandfather's lap and went to the basket near the fireplace to add more firewood but found it empty. He tiptoed through the house to not wake anyone and gently opened the front door to retrieve the firewood from the basket outside. He quickly stepped out and picked up the bundle he'd added earlier. A heavy footstep on the floorboards behind him had the child spinning around quickly, only to see his grandfather smiling at him and holding his finger to his lips. He whispered, "Shh, it's just pop-pop. What do you have there? Firewood? Great, come, let's go warm everyone inside with a nice fire, and we can tuck you into bed, okay?" He extended his hand, and his grandchild reached out and grabbed him with a single finger.

They gently closed the door behind them and crept through the house. The child mimicked his grandfather's movements as he tiptoed and moved slowly through the house. They both stooped at the fireplace; the child, still holding onto his grandfather's finger, handed him piece by piece of firewood to add to

KRAMPUS

the fireplace.

"Come on, my little gumdrop. Let's get you tucked away in bed," the old man remarked. He stood up and turned to walk to the stairs. The child sprang to his feet with the help of his grandfather, lifting him by his arm. But confusion was etched on the old man's face when the child moved from an upright position to hanging horizontally while still holding his hand. The old man looked at the child's feet and screamed when his eyes fell on a hand wrapped around the ankle of the child. It yanked him off his feet and up the fireplace. The old man's shriek alerted everyone. They woke up to find the old man with his hand up the fireplace chimney and the child's screams filling the house. His grandfather shouted his name and cried out in fright.

A demonic howl slithered down the chimney, a deep, bellowing growl before a beast's high-pitched howl. They heard the sound of chains rattling inside the chimney and the blood-curdling screams of the child as his grandfather began to lose his grip, "Papa! Don't let go, Papa!"

The old man's children sprang into action. The child's mother and father reached in over the burning firewood and stuck their hands inside the fireplace chimney to grab onto their son. The three of them grabbed hold of him and pulled him back. Another beastly howl echoed through the house, extinguishing the fireplace's fire. The old man looked up the chimney, and the illuminated eyes of the beast bouncing the light off the chimney walls lit up its face. Its jaws unhinged and opened a maw that was almost as wide as the chimney. Krampus bit off the child's hand that they had a hold-off, and all three tumbled backward out of the chimney. The child's screams ceased within a few seconds of them hitting the ground. In its place, blood rained down onto the fireplace and sizzled on the hot pieces of timber.

Silence filled the room for a brief moment. The old man crawled on his hands and knees and looked up the chimney again, yelling out his grandchild's name. Blood dripped onto his face, and soon after, the child's remains fell onto the fireplace. Noticing the hand of the child on the ground, they all began screaming as the blood started flowing down the bricks of the chimney and onto the floor. The sound of chains rattling and one last howl was heard that night as both sounds moved away and soon could not be heard again.

CHAPTER

2

Two weeks later, the house was sold for next to nothing. The family was too shaken by that night's events and couldn't bear another night in the house where they would forever remember the worst night of their lives. Fresh out of college, Alister October had hit the jackpot and won the lottery. He'd found an amazing deal on the internet for a home in a secluded location; it was an hour's drive from a rural farming town at the base of the hill. Alister bought the house on a whim; its location and set-up were perfect for him: it was away from people and quiet. He enjoyed writing, but peace and quiet were hard to find living in a house with multiple families. Alister was the eldest of his cousins and uncle to several nieces and nephews, so somehow, distractions always found him. Using the small fortune he'd come into, Alister invested in his own little slice of paradise away from everyone. No one knew about his stroke of luck. He figured people would bring their financial burdens to him when all he wanted was to be left alone to do the things he liked and work on himself and his career.

Even though Alister didn't like people, he loved his family. One day he overheard them refusing to go on vacation because of their kids. So, he decided to book them into a nice hotel and pay for a mini getaway during the Christmas holiday. He also planned to offer to watch the kids and hang out with his cousins at his new house. He told everyone that it belonged to a friend who had loaned it to him for the holidays and that he was happy to babysit his nieces and nephews with his cousins while they went on vacation for a few days. The only people who knew the truth were his closest cousins, Ravi and James.

Knowing he was a responsible uncle to the

children, they felt comfortable leaving them with him for a few days since he had been babysitting them and his younger cousins most of their lives.

On December 23rd, the October family gathered at the airport. Two separate flights were boarded that day, one to the Caribbean and the other to Switzerland. The adults would relax for a few days in the tropics before joining Alister and the others in Switzerland for Christmas. After a long goodbye from the adults, Alister and company boarded their plane and were off to Switzerland.

The group of six landed at the Zurich Airport. Alister made them group together to ensure everyone was there. "Alright, come over and hold my hand when I call your name. Then the next person will come and hold their hand, and so forth; you guys know the drill," he said with a smile. The group looked at him and nodded, 'Yes.'

"Okay, starting from the youngest, Alyssa," Alister called out.

Alyssa walked over and held his hand. "Here," she replied.

"Very good, okay; next is Shay," Alister

continued.

Shay walked over and held Alyssa's hand.

"Very nice, and the last little one, Benji," said Alister.

Benji walked over and held Shay's hand.

"And the cousins, Ravi and James," said Alister.

"And Alister!" Benji chimed in.

Alister chuckled, "That's right, Benji."

The group held hands and walked to the exit. There a driver awaited them, holding up a sign labeled 'October.' Alister waved at the man and led the others to him. Huddling into a seven-seater minivan, Alister and James had packed their bags into the trunk while Ravi helped the kids get seated. Ravi sat in front with the driver while Alister and James got in the back with the kids and were off. They embarked on a sixty-mile drive to the Swiss Alps, just outside the mountain village of Wengen.

The two-and-a-half-hour drive put the kids to sleep on the way. Alister and James sat on their phones, taking pictures of the beautiful scenery in Switzerland on the way. Ravi was suddenly a bit chatty; Alister and James were stunned that he understood and spoke a little German and French.

"Since when can you speak another language?" Alister chuckled.

"I've been here before; you pick it up after a while," Ravi explained.

"We grew up in the same house; when did you visit Switzerland? Much less stay long enough to learn to speak it?" questioned Alister.

"I met people here, stayed in touch, and learned little by little. At least enough to get by—" Ravi exclaimed.

"Oh, you mean that girl you always talk about? What was her name?" asked James.

"Adelheid, yeah, that's her," said Ravi.

"We've got kids with us; keep your 'extracurricular' activities away from them if she comes to see you," Alister chuckled.

"Sure thing, dad," Ravi laughed. "Don't worry about it. I will go see her; she said it's quite a walk up that hill where we will be staying. I wouldn't ask that of her," said Ravi.

"You're such a gentleman," James teased.

Ravi raised his hand above the seat and stuck his

middle finger up at the giggling duo behind him.

The driver pulled up at the house. The cousins excitedly exited the car and inhaled that fresh mountain air. The view was stunning; the house was even more impressive in person. Alister could not believe he'd gotten such an amazing deal with this. He felt like the luckiest person alive, first the lottery and now this stunning house in a place he'd always wanted to go to. Alister was lost for words; he sat on the green grass dusted with snow and felt the cold leaves through his fingers and the wintry mountain air beating on his skin.

Ravi and James unpacked the bags from the minivan. Alister got up and took his nieces and nephew inside. Still asleep, he held all three of them and placed them on the sofa near the fireplace. Hurrying back out to help Ravi and James with the bags, Alister paid the driver, and they all went back inside.

CHAPTER

3

Alister and James made their way through the house, cleaning and rearranging it to their liking. Thankfully, before they had gotten there, the house was cleaned top to bottom by the sellers, so not much needed to be done. They both joined Ravi outside, who was checking out the garage and its contents. They found him going through old boxes the previous owners had left behind. "Find anything interesting?" asked Alister as he walked into the garage.

"Just a bunch of random stuff, really... Old clothes, broken items, nothing of value," Ravi replied.

James noticed a black leather book in one of the boxes. He reached in, took it out, and flipped through. "Oh, I've already gone through that. It's just a log of the jobs done, mostly collecting firewood. It's sort of the day-to-day stuff the owners did here," Ravi explained.

"There are more of them," Alister said as he picked up three more books. "These date back to twenty-eighteen; that's four years ago." He browsed through the old books, each containing the same type of information: a schedule for getting firewood and other provisions. Sometimes, the person would list out when there was a drop in temperature or any events that took place which he felt were worth taking note of.

"Must have been an old guy; my stepdad used to do this all the time. He said it was a way to keep his mind active," Ravi exclaimed.

"How is the old man?" Alister enquired while still flipping through the pages of the books.

"I haven't heard from him since last month. The last time we spoke, he told me he had a job to do and would be out of the country for a few days. I tried calling, but I didn't even get a ring," Ravi answered.

"Maybe it's a signal thing? I mean, I'm not really getting much reception up here, but the internet works fine," Alister stated.

"Don't you usually tag along when he takes work trips?" asked James.

"Usually, but this time he just went ahead without me. Kinda worked out, though. Normally, I would've been bored from hanging out in hotel rooms alone while he's away," Ravi explained.

"Do you guys remember when he took us to a gun range and taught us how to shoot?" Alister asked.

"Or the camping trips where we had to live off the land," James added.

"That guy did more things with us than our real dads," Ravi exclaimed.

"That's an understatement," Alister chuckled.

James dropped the book back into the box and looked at them. "Well, we've got a lot of nature out here. There's no other house in sight, just a hill and some woods, and the kids will be asleep for a bit longer. Let's go explore like the old days," James suggested.

"You guys go on ahead if you want. I don't want to leave the kids here alone," Alister commented.

"It's about a five-minute walk to the woods. What do you think is going to happen? There is nobody here except for us," exclaimed James.

"This is why they don't leave you in charge," Alister chuckled.

"Lighten up, man. We used to be left alone all the time when we were kids," said James.

"And you broke your hand playing on a log, and somehow, to this day, I get blamed for that," Alister replied, shaking his head in laughter. "I don't want something happening to them, and then I get blamed for that too!"

"Fair enough, but you did break my hand, though," said James.

"You rolled off a log and fell backward on your hand. All three of us did, so how is that my fault?" Alister questioned. James couldn't contain his laughter.

"Alright, we'll go on ahead. When the kids wake up, you can meet up with us. I wanna see what's at the top of the hill," James exclaimed.

"Yeah, I want to see that, too," Ravi chimed in.

"Sounds good. Maybe you can get some firewood while you're out there. The last owner always kept some on hand," Alister advised.

"I'm sure we can find an axe or something around here," said Ravi.

"Not 'it!'" James called out.

"Fine. I'll cut; you carry," Ravi replied.

"I want to change my answer," James exclaimed.

"Nope, too late," answered Ravi.

"Why not?" whined James.

"I'm older," said Ravi.

"I'm bigger," James responded, flexing his biceps.

"Good, then you can carry the wood back," Ravi replied, tapping his arms before walking off to look for an axe.

Alister shook his head and laughed at them, bickering. Looking down at the boxes, he placed all the books into one box and took them inside.

James and Ravi found a basket and an axe they could use to gather the firewood. Alister stood in the kitchen and watched as they walked up the hill and into the woods. Sitting near the fireplace, he leafed through the books he'd found in the garage. "If I'm going to live here, I'll need to learn how things work. There's not exactly a convenience store nearby where I can pick up household items," he mumbled to himself.

Alister flipped through each page, carefully beginning with the first book of the four.

CHAPTER

4

Ravi and James hiked through the woods. They were covered in several layers of jackets and shirts to keep warm against the cold winds at six degrees Celsius. Neither of them was a stranger to the cold weather; they preferred it to warmer conditions. Ravi had strapped the axe over his shoulder, while James had the backpack-like basket on his back. "What do you think we could use for firewood out here?" asked James.

"I see a lot of pine trees and some evergreen. My stepdad always used birch or oak when we went camping, so keep an eye out for those," Ravi replied.

"I'm a little rusty. I haven't been out camping since we were little. I know what evergreens and pine trees look like, but I couldn't point out a birch, to be honest," James responded.

"Well, this is the Alps. A lot of different trees grow here. Evergreens typically grow near the border of the Alps, and I can't recall what maple looks like. But birch is easy to spot: the trees with white bark. Keep an eye out for that," Ravi explained.

"Hey, how do you know so much about this stuff?" asked James.

Ravi trekked ahead, looking around in different directions. "My stepdad... I have some obscured bits of knowledge thanks to him, you know? Growing up, he taught me different things, stuff like this, and then some even weirder things," Ravi answered.

"What kind of weird things?" James enquired.

"Well, when I was a kid, he told me that there were certain things you always needed around the house or on you: silver, salt, iron, holy water... He said it wards off evil and protects you," Ravi replied.

"That's so random," James commented.

"Well, for context, I used to be afraid of a lot of things. I was even scared of my own shadow. So, he made me a little keychain with everything he'd told me about, and I've kept it on my person ever since. I'm not going to lie; it made me feel better. I often felt scared and spooked, especially when I was alone. But since I got the keychain, I don't feel that way anymore," said Ravi as he reached into his pocket, took out said keychain, and raised it for James to see.

"Oh, this is cool: a mini silver sword, two mini mason jars with salt and holy water, a mini iron crowbar... Yo, this is neat, man," James replied. "It's so weird. We've always seen you with the keychain but never really paid attention to what was on it."

"I know, right. I always thought it was pretty cool. He even taught me how to make holy water," Ravi exclaimed.

"What? Really?" James said, shocked.

"For sure... He and my mom were really superstitious. It's kinda how they met; both of them were buying items they could use to 'cleanse' the house of evil and stuff at the supermarket, and they just hit it off," Ravi responded.

"That's pretty cool. We know Aunty is really into star signs and Mercury in retrograde and all that. The rest of them aren't into that kind of stuff," said James.

"With mom, sometimes it gets to be a bit much. She still believes that if you break a mirror or a black cat crosses your path, you will get back luck. Do you know she never gives someone pepper in their hand? She places it on a surface and lets them pick it up. She thinks that if you hand someone a pepper, you and that person will argue. It's like, come on... You're too old to believe in those things to the point where it alters your life," Ravi stated.

"I mean, people believe what they do because it brings them comfort. Try to find some deeper meaning in it. It's what having faith is," James commented.

"Faith, I can accept, but if you tell me that when you wake up, the stars tell you how to feel that day, then that's too much," Ravi chuckled.

***

Alister sat with the books on the sofa. His youngest niece, Alyssa, now awake, sat up on the sofa and looked at him with sleepy eyes. He closed the book and moved over next to her, "Wakey, wakey, doll."

Alister put his arm around her. Alyssa hugged his arm and leaned on him, her eyes drooping back to sleep.

Alister was sitting between all three of the kids. Each woke up and snuggled closer to him, and Alister eventually fell asleep together with them. Slipping in and out of sleep, Alister began drifting into a deep slumber when he was startled awake by the sound of dragging chains. His head lifted off the sofa, and he looked around. Alister listened for a moment but didn't hear anything afterward. He dismissed it as something he'd heard in his head or maybe dreamt, which startled him. He closed his eyes and tried to go back to sleep.

Suddenly, the quiet of the room was broken. A crackling sound coming from the chimney forced Alister's eyes open. Curious, he turned his attention to the fireplace. Standing up, he exhaled a frosty breath. The temperature had dropped several degrees in an instant. The crackling sound coming from the chimney above the fireplace intensified. Alister moved closer toward it, and there he saw icicles forming down the bricks.

Alister turned around, ran into the upstairs bedrooms, and got extra blankets for the kids. He noticed the rooms were equipped with heat and immediately took the kids to the room. He turned up the heat to keep them warm and tucked them gently into bed. Benji woke up and yawned.

"Hey, bud, it's okay. Go back to sleep," Alister whispered.

"What's going on?" Benji asked while stretching.

"I'm going to get some firewood with Uncle James and Uncle Ravi. While I'm gone, I'm leaving you in charge, okay? You're the oldest, so you need to protect your cousins. Lock the door when I leave this room, and do not open it until we get back," said Alister. "Can you do that for me?"

"Yes," answered Benji.

"Tell me again what you need to do," said Alister.

"Lock the door, and don't open it unless it's for Uncle. I am in charge until you get back," said Benji quietly.

"You're forgetting something very important," Alister replied.

"Protect Alyssa and Shay?" Benji asked.

"That's right. More than anything else, you have to keep them safe. You're strong, okay? We won't be far, just a bit up the hill. If anything goes wrong, I want you to shout as loud as you can, okay?" said Alister.

"Yes," Benji replied.

"Can I count on you to look after your cousins?" Alister repeated.

"Yes, I can do this," Benji replied.

Alister ruffled his hair and kissed the top of his head, "That's my little warrior. Okay, we will be quick. We just need some wood for the fire; the house is getting really cold, and we don't want you guys getting sick. I'll be quick." Alister got up and walked out the door, closing it behind him. He waited for a few seconds; he heard the shuffling of little feet running to the door, followed by the click of the door being locked. He smiled, grabbed an extra jacket, and hurried out the front door.

Alister took one look outside and saw it was as dark as night.

CHAPTER

5

Alister was baffled; there should have been a couple hours left before nightfall. Stepping outside, he looked up, and his eyes met dark clouds. His body trembled as a gust of blistering cold winds blew past him. "Oh, what the hell!" he gasped and shrugged his shoulders. "I see why they always made sure they had firewood."

Alister took out his phone and switched on the phone's flashlight. He used this to guide his way as he hurried into the woods.

***

James and Ravi had chopped down a birch tree and had just finished cutting it into pieces to carry back. With an axe in hand, Ravi swung strongly to split apart the last piece of the tree and placed it in the basket on James' back. "I think we should be good for now," Ravi informed James.

"How long have we been out here? It's already dark out!" James commented as he looked at his watch. The time read ten past four. "You're the Swiss expert. Does it usually get dark this early?" he inquired.

"It shouldn't be this dark for at least another hour and a half. It must be due to some bad weather. I'm actually starting to lose feeling in my fingertips," Ravi answered.

"Alright, let's go back with what we have," James replied when a loud thump behind them drew their attention.

"What the hell was that?" Ravi asked, wielding his axe. "Hey! Is anybody out there!? Alister, is that you?"

Ravi and James backed away slowly, keeping their gaze focused on the direction of the sound they'd heard. Suddenly they heard the sound of chains being dragged on the ground. The visibility in the woods started to fade, and a thick fog began to blanket the woods.

"James, let's get out of here!" Ravi suggested as he pulled James by his shoulder to turn him toward the house.

"Yeah, right behind you," James agreed.

Ravi and James hurried back toward the house. At one point, James turned his head and glimpsed something on the tree beside him. He saw a large bony hand wrapping around the trunk of the tree. James shrieked and fell over as he jumped away from the tree. Ravi turned immediately and looked around frantically, his axe raised and ready to strike.

"What? What is it?" asked Ravi, hurrying over to James.

"I saw a hand; something was behind the tree!" James spat.

"Where!?" questioned Ravi, tightening his grip on the axe.

James pointed to the tree. Ravi turned and slowly inched toward it, ready to swing his axe. A low bellowing growl emerged from behind the tree. Ravi froze for a moment in fear; his hands began to tremble, and his knees began to shake. He mustered his strength, took a step closer, held the axe tight, and raised it to strike.

There was movement behind the trees; loud thumps on the ground could be heard as the creature walked out from behind the treeline. Ravi rushed in to strike but found a goat with its head pointed to the ground as it ate. He withheld his swing and laughed hysterically. "It's just a goat. You got scared of a goat!" Ravi snickered as he turned, walked over to James, and helped him off the ground.

"That's not what I saw. I saw a hand, man. I know a hand when I see one!" James declared.

"Maybe it was the pattern on the tree bark? They kinda look like branches, so you might have mistaken it for a hand. But it's just a little goat back there," Ravi responded. He began picking up the fallen pieces of firewood from the floor and re-filled the basket.

"Little? Man, take a closer look. That thing is almost as tall as us on all fours!" James ranted.

"You're right. Wow, that's some big pieces of

lamb chops," Ravi commented, licking his lips.

"That's a goat, you idiot, not a lamb," James corrected.

"You know what I mean," Ravi countered.

"Its horns look weird. It almost looks like antlers," James mused.

"I'm not a zoologist, but I know the mountain goats here look different than what we are used to seeing," Ravi replied.

"Come on, let's just go. I'm starting to freeze here," said James.

"Wait, wait. Let's get a picture with the goat," Ravi suggested.

"Seriously?" James replied.

"Come on, one quick selfie," Ravi answered excitedly. Taking his phone out of his pocket, he raised it above them and took a picture of them and the goat.

The flash went off, indicating the picture was captured. When the sound of chains was heard again, Ravi and James turned around, but the goat was gone. "Good, you scared it," James commented.

"Yuck, that thing really stunk. It smelled horrible; let's just go," James said as they both walked off. Their feet crunched the leaves on the ground as they disappeared into the darkness. At the base of the tree where the goat had been lay the remains of a human skull and chunks of flesh. A large hoof stepped on the skull, crushing it to bits. Draped in a thick dark cloth dragging on the ground with chains and bones tethered onto it, the creature moved away swiftly, its deep growl fading into the woods.

CHAPTER

6

Alister marched up the hill and through the woods. Using his phone as a flashlight to see the path, he periodically called out to James and Ravi. On the next step he took, he heard a loud crunch under his feet. Alister raised his boot and flashed the phone's light on the ground. He stooped to the ground to get a closer look and found a Christmas ornament broken to pieces. "A Christmas tree ornament? What is that doing all the way in the woods?" he wondered.

Suddenly, Alister heard Ravi and James coming down the hill, mumbling and bickering like they usually do. He quickly waved the phone's light to get their attention.

"Alister?" James called out, squinting and covering his eyes from the bright light.

"Over here, guys. Did you get the firewood? The house is starting to freeze," Alister exclaimed.

"Where are the kids?" asked James.

"They are locked in the bedroom. The bedrooms are the only rooms with heat," Alister replied.

"After all that talk about being Mr. Responsible, huh, James," Ravi joked.

"It's freezing out here. I couldn't possibly bring them out here when it's this cold! Besides, they're asleep. Benji woke up before I left, so I told him to make sure they didn't leave that room until we got back. We should get moving now," Alister advised.

"Wait, what's that?" asked James, pointing to the ground near Alister's feet.

"It's a broken ornament," Alister replied.

"No, not that, genius. Look inside," said James as he stooped down and pulled a piece of paper from the shards of the broken Christmas ornament.

James unfolded the wrinkled piece of cloth-like

paper, and Alister flashed the light to see it clearer. Alister pulled the paper closer and read the message, which was still wet on the cloth. "He sees you when you're sleeping…," he read out loud before looking up at Ravi and James. "Guys… This ink is still wet."

"I don't think that's ink. Notice how it's red but darker and almost black in spots? If I didn't know any better, I would say that's… Blood," Ravi surmised, touching the ink and holding his finger in the light.

"Let's get back to the house…," said James.

Alister looked at the horror on James' face while James and Ravi briefly exchanged glances. They took off running to the house. Alister sprinted behind them, passing them and running ahead, making it out of the woods first. Alister's heart began racing when he saw the silhouette of a hand inside the bedroom window where he'd left the kids. Benji and the others screamed out loud, and the light in the room went dark.

Alister called out to Benji as he burst through the door and rushed up the stairs. He ran to their door, banging on it vigorously and shouting for Benji to unlock it. Alister continued to hear their screams in the room. He tried to kick down the door but was unable to do so. Acting quickly, he ran into the room next door, opened the window, and jumped out onto the roof. He rushed over to the kids' window but found them joyfully playing and screaming in the room together.

Alister looked around from his spot outside the window and saw nobody else but the kids in the room. He let out a sigh of relief and leaned against the wall. For a moment, he had thought something had happened to them. Taking a few seconds to compose himself, he knocked on the window and called out to Benji. Benji quickly came over and unlocked the window for him just as Ravi and James returned to the house.

"What are you doing up there?!" asked James, panting and leaning over winded.

"The door was locked, and I couldn't get in," Alister replied right before he slipped through the window. He quickly huddled the kids together and embraced them. "That's the last time I'm leaving you guys alone," he mumbled.

"What did you say?" asked Alyssa.

"It's nothing, doll. Don't worry about it. Are you guys having fun?" Alister remarked.

They all shook their heads yes and smiled

energetically.

"Good, good. Well, we've got the firewood, so we can warm up in a bit while watching Christmas movies. Now, who wants hot chocolate?" asked Alister.

"Me!" they all shouted.

"Okay, come on. Let's go build that fire, and I will get you your hot chocolates. Sounds good?" Alister enquired. "Okay, girls, you go down and help Uncle Ravi and Uncle James build a fire. Benji, you're coming with me. We are going to make sure all the windows are locked, okay?"

"Okay," Benji replied.

Alyssa and Shay ran downstairs. James and Ravi were throwing the smaller pieces of wood onto the grate to start the fire before they went to cut the other pieces into more reasonable sizes.

Seeing Alyssa coming down the stairs, James told her to bring the lighter from the kitchen. Shay trailed her, and they both went into the kitchen to retrieve the lighter. After several failed attempts, they finally got the firewood to light. James went outside and to the side of the house, where he chopped the rest of the wood. A much thicker fog began to settle; the floor was almost invisible. James began chopping the pieces of wood. Meanwhile, Alister and Benji went around to every room and locked the windows. Ravi and the girls were at the fireplace warming up when he noticed a rack of old newspapers. He used them to stoke the fire hot until James returned with the firewood.

James broke apart the wood easily. Swinging with great force, his jacket sleeve hugged his massive biceps tightly with each swing. Placing the last piece to be chopped on the ground, James took his last swing and split the piece of wood without any struggle. He looked up and exhaled deeply after finishing.

Dead ahead, just at the edge of the woods, James noticed two luminous eyes peering through the darkness and the fog and looking right at him. James tightened his grip on the axe and looked on, keeping his eyes on the creature in the woods. The sound of chains behind him startled him, but when he turned, nobody was there. He quickly turned his attention back to the woods, but the eyes had disappeared. The fog grew thicker, and soon, he couldn't see the woods clearly. James quickly piled the wood in the basket and went inside. He took one last look at the woods before opening the door and stepping inside.

CHAPTER

7

The dark night matured as time flew by. Alister, James, and the kids sat in the living room around the warm fire, watching classic Christmas cartoons. Ravi was pacing around the room upstairs, talking to Adelheid via social media since there was no signal strong enough to maintain a phone call. But minutes had passed, and he still didn't get a response from her. Ravi grew uneasy. Soon after, the power went out. He looked out the window to the view of Wengen in the distance down the hill. Like a wave of shadows crashing over the village, the specs of light peeping through the fog had now vanished from the village.

Alister had come prepared. As a writer, he was always paranoid about losing his work in the event of a blackout or power surge. Usually, he would have several backups on hand to keep working in such a situation. And in extreme cases, it would give him enough time to save his progress before shutting down his laptop. He went into his bags and brought out several power supply devices. He connected the television and the Wi-Fi router so that they would still be able to watch their shows and connect to the internet. James helped him set up the television on the power supply before leaving the kids sitting in front of the television to watch a movie. Alister and James then rummaged through the house, looking for candles.

Searching through the kitchen drawers, they had no luck finding candles, but they got their hands on two large LED flashlights. "Wow, look at this. This is heavy. Bro, would the people who lived here really leave all this stuff? This house is fully stocked, man," James commented.

"It's beyond me. This almost feels unreal, bro. I got this house for less money than it would take to buy a new car," Alister replied.

"Speaking of, man, when are you going to tell the family about this? Are you just going to say goodbye when we all return to the airport, and they realize you aren't boarding the plane with us?" asked James.

"I'll tell them, but the guilt, the questions, and the drama it would bring are what I don't want to deal with that right now. I just want to be left alone, you know?" Alister answered.

"I get that. I know it hasn't been a picnic growing up with our family, but what can you do?" James responded.

"Well, for one, I can move out and away from everyone so I can get a little peace," said Alister as he chuckled.

"Come on, man. I'm serious," James countered.

"So am I. This isn't some complicated situation. It's not about hatred or dislike or anything like that. All I want is peace; I want to wake up naturally without someone screaming first thing in the morning. I want to go one day without hearing about someone's grudges against someone else. I want to be away from the bickering and drama. None of that means I don't love my family. It's just what I want. I made this choice for myself without putting anyone else first. That's all it is," Alister explained.

"And what about your nieces? What about Benji, me, and Ravi? Are we supposed to be okay with the fact that when we go home, we won't see you again?" James shot back.

"You've got phones, don't you? We can talk anytime you want, and we can video chat. I can come to visit you, and you can come to visit me. You and the kids are always welcome here, you know that," said Alister.

"Except that here is a couple thousand miles away, and you know we don't have that kind of money to make so many trips. Even if we put aside that much to come here to visit, we can't do that often, maybe twice a year. I am not okay with that, man," James stated.

"Come on, James," said Alister.

"No, that's not good enough. You are like a brother to me. We've been through everything together, and you're just leaving everything behind, including me," James retorted.

"He has a point," Ravi agreed as he entered the kitchen. "How could you do this to us, man? You did all this without us? We don't even get a say?"

Alister looked at them both, "That's enough, both of you. I'm tired, man. I really am. I caught a break, and I took it and ran with it. I will not apologize for looking out for me. I've looked out for my family for as long as I can remember. Hell, I raised both of you. I was there when you were babies and crying alone. I woke up endless nights with you. I skipped out on partying and having my own life because I gave my all for my family, and I loved every minute of it. We were kids running around, playing pirates and witches. We went ghost hunting in the middle of the night when everyone fell asleep. We used that app that told you that a ghost was near you on radar and hid in the dark to find something with an infrared camera on a tablet.

"We did everything together, and if I had a chance to do it all over again, I would go back in a heartbeat because back then, life was simple. We played and laughed, and life was nothing but fun. But that fairy tale ended. We grew up, got our own friends, our own lives, responsibilities, and life happened. And

I got the short end of the stick. I learned the hard way that life will not treat you better because you are a good person, and when push comes to shove, people will always look out for themselves first. All I did was make that decision too. Don't stand here and guilt-trip me for putting myself first for once," Alister said.

James and Ravi looked down and scratched their heads. "It's just hard to lose someone you love," James muttered.

"Come on, man. Don't get all mushy on me," Alister chuckled. "You didn't lose anything. I'll always be there for you guys. Always."

"I guess we can't change your mind about this, huh?" said Ravi.

"Not really. As I said, it's not about hatred or anything. It's just something I did solely for me, nobody else. I get that it will hurt the people around me, but I can't bleed because everyone else is bleeding. Otherwise, we would all die," Alister replied. "I want to start living for me, you know?"

"I guess," James responded sadly.

"On that note, I need to go and see Adelheid," said Ravi.

"What? Why?" asked Alister.

"It didn't just black out here. Wengen went dark too, and I hadn't heard from her in a while before the power went. Last I heard, she was home alone, so I'm gonna go drop in," Ravi explained.

"You're going to walk two miles downhill in the freezing cold during a blackout to see a girl you met once?" James enquired.

"You ever wonder why her nickname is Heidi? Well, it's because I hid my—" Ravi began before Alister covered his mouth.

"Nah ah ah, we really don't need to hear the rest of that. Here, take this," Alister said and handed him one of the flashlights.

"Be careful; the fog is really thick out there," James said.

"See you guys in a couple hours. I should be home before midnight," said Ravi as he threw on a jacket and left.

CHAPTER

8

Alister and James looked through the kitchen window, watching Ravi as he headed out into the night with the flashlight. "Bro, that is really bright. It's almost like daylight in front of him," James commented.

"You know, I've heard of these. It's somewhere in the area of one hundred thousand lumens. Damn," Alister responded.

"I just searched how bright our phone's flashlight is, and it's only fifty lumens on the high end. Put that into perspective!" said James.

"Sheesh, that's crazy. I like these flashlights. It's so heavy with a fully aluminum body. It really does beg the question, why did the owners leave something like this back?" stated Alister.

"Why did they sell anyway?" James asked.

"When I contacted the seller, I spoke to an older gentleman. He didn't even heckle me for a price. If anything, he pushed the sale on me. He didn't really state his reason for selling," Alister replied.

"You think it's because it's so far removed from anything else? I mean, the nearest village is two miles downhill," James exclaimed.

"Well, there is a garage, so maybe he had a vehicle?" said Alister.

"An ordinary car can't make it up that hill. You'll need a serious four-wheel drive to make it up that trail. A car doing that often is sure to wear out quickly," James stated.

"Good point. And that garage isn't big enough for a truck. Maybe he used it as a storage space?" Alister mused.

"That would make sense," James agreed.

"Well, I'm just glad I got it. This place is great,"

Alister exclaimed.

"About that, man…," James began.

"What?" asked Alister.

"When we were out in the woods, I think I saw something. It really freaked me out," James continued.

"What did you see?" Alister enquired.

"I heard chains dragging on the ground, and I saw a hand wrapped around a tree," James answered.

"A hand? Tell me something, was it kinda bony with long fingers?" asked Alister.

James looked at Alister and froze for a moment, "Yeah… How did you know that?"

"James… When I ran out to check on the kids through the bedroom window, I saw the shadow of a hand, and it looked like that," Alister explained.

"That's not all…," said James. He paused briefly and looked around to ensure the kids were not nearby. "When I was chopping firewood, I saw something in the woods. It looked like eyes, but it was white and almost glowing. I heard the chains right behind me, but when I turned around, there was nothing there, and the eyes in the woods had disappeared," James continued.

"Did you tell Ravi?" Alister asked.

"He was right there when it happened, but when he checked, he found a goat," James remarked.

Alister shook his head in confusion. "A goat? That's so random," he said. "Do you think it was the goat in the woods and just the eyes reflecting back at you?"

"It wasn't reflecting; it was like a glow. The eyes were emitting light. I know I saw a hand, and I think you saw it too," said James.

"I believe you; I know what I saw, too," Alister stated.

"Do you think we shouldn't have let Ravi go out there?" asked James worriedly.

"We couldn't stop him even if we wanted to. We're adults now. I can't tell him what he can and cannot do. I'm the oldest, but I don't call the shots," said Alister.

"If anything happened to him, I don't think I could live with myself," James claimed.

"Relax. Come on, do you know who his stepdad is? You've seen that guy. He is a badass, and Ravi is the carbon copy of that guy. Of any of us, Ravi is surely the toughest. You're the strongest, and I'm just

51

somewhere in the middle with more experience," Alister replied.

"I guess," said James.

"Don't worry; he's got his protection charm, man. He said that works, so let's have some faith in him. Come on, let's go spend some time with the kids," Alister suggested.

Alister and James strolled out of the kitchen with the flashlight in hand and sat next to the kids on the sofa. James watched the movie with the kids, but Alister was buried in his phone, scrolling the internet.

***

Ravi trekked down the hill. After a grueling half-hour walk through the icy winds and fog, the temperature raised significantly. Ravi stepped out of the fog and turned back. The bad weather had stopped abruptly further down the hill. Ravi stuck his hand out into the fog and felt the chill in the air. It was like sticking his hand in the freezer. "That's a new one…," he mumbled. He turned and kept walking down the hill. Dark heavy clouds were still settled above the land, with no sign of power for as far as he could have seen.

Ravi soon got a swarm of messages, including

missed calls. The messages were all from Adelheid, and most of the calls were from her, but among them, Ravi saw his stepdad had left a few calls. He tried calling his step-dad's phone. It barely rang once before a woman answered his phone. "Ravi? Ravi is that you?" she asked.

Ravi tried to place the voice for a moment. "Heidi! Heidi, is that you?" Ravi asked, stunned.

"It's me," answered Adelheid.

"Heidi, why do you have my dad's phone?" Ravi questioned.

"He left it in case you called. Ravi, where are you right now?" asked Adelheid.

"I'm about just over an hour away from Wengen. I'm on my way to you now," Ravi replied.

"No…" she gasped.

"Heidi, what's wrong?" Ravi responded in a deeply concerned tone.

"Ravi, you need to get inside now. It's not sa… Ou….. Ere." The signal broke on Adelheid's call, and soon after, Ravi heard the beep of the call ending.

Ravi turned back to the house and looked into the thick fog. "What is dad doing here?" he wondered. Ravi ignored her words and ran down to the village with the flashlight in hand.

CHAPTER

9

In the village of Wengen, Adelheid sat in her house trying to call Ravi after their call had disconnected. At this time, the temperature had begun to drop, and icicles started forming on the windows and doors. Fog seeped through under the doors, covering the floor of Adelheid's house. She tried looking out the window into the darkness of the village, but the ice had spread and covered the window, obstructing her view of the outside. A loud thump on her roof, accompanied by chains rattling, averted her gaze skyward.

Adelheid looked up at the ceiling, and with her

eyes, she followed the sound of the stomps as they moved across her roof. She soon realized it was heading for the chimney. When it took that last step just above the chimney, it caused dust to fall down the fireplace and onto the flame. A low blood-curdling growl then echoed down the chimney and into the house. Adelheid's scream pierced the quiet village. Ravi, who was just outside of the town, heard her. He picked up the pace and rushed over to her house.

Adelheid grabbed a bottle of lighter fluid and flooded the fireplace. The massive flame shot up the chimney; the glow of the fire could be seen coming out the top. Ravi stopped dead in his tracks a short distance from her house. The subtle orange glow shone a light on a creature standing atop her roof, cloaked in a dark robe, with horns like antlers towering over its massive body. A skull face with eyes that glowed white peered down the chimney before howling.

The creature's howl blew out the flames of the fireplace. Adelheid's scream that followed this broke Ravi out of his frozen state. He rushed to the house without thinking about it, calling out to her as he did so. Hearing him, she ran to the door and tried opening it, but to no avail. The ice had settled over the door and frozen it shut. Ravi made it to the front door and tried opening it but ultimately failed as she did. "Heidi!" he screamed.

"Ravi! I can't get it open," Adelheid shouted.

"Stand back!" Ravi yelled. Taking a few steps back, he tried to kick down the door. Another howl down the fireplace sent a gust of wind through the house. Adelheid turned around, her hair fluttering from the force of the creature's roar. Krampus' horns slowly peeked out of the fireplace; his long bony fingers held onto the sides as he pulled himself through. His hooves stomped on the ground as he slowly stood, reaching well over six feet tall. The sound of Ravi trying to kick the door down slowly faded away as Adelheid stood, shaking in fear in the presence of Krampus. The skull face unhinged its jaw, which opened two feet wide, and she could see a black goo holding the jaw to the skull. The light in Krampus' eyes went dark. Suddenly, Adelheid's eyes turned over into her head, exposing only the whites as her body was unable to move.

Ravi rammed into the door with his body, crashing through and into the house. The creature turned to him, and its eyes lit up once more. Heidi's eyes returned to normal as she gasped for air. "What the fuck is that?" Ravi exclaimed.

"Exorcizamus te, omnis immundus spiritus. Omnis Satanica potestas, omnis incursio infernalis adversii..." Ravi chanted.

Krampus charged at Ravi; the force of the impact sent Ravi flying through the door and rolling into the yard outside. Ravi held his chest and coughed. Gasping for air, his eyes opened only to see the creature's maw widely spread above him. A deep growl escaped its lips as it leaned down toward him. A shotgun cocked, and the creature looked up just as the trigger had been pulled. It swiftly ran off into the night, howling in pain, seemingly disappearing into thin air as it leaped several feet into the air.

Rushing to his side, Ravi's stepfather kneeled beside him and helped him off the ground. "Ravi? Ravi, is that you?" he exclaimed.

"Dad? What are you doing here?" Ravi muttered.

"Mister Raphael, thank God," said Adelheid from the door.

"Get up, son. We can't stay out here," Raphael

stated as he picked Ravi off the ground, and they both rushed into the house.

"Ravi, why are you in Wengen, son? You need to answer me. Now!" Raphael demanded.

"Um, I came with Alister, James, and the kids. We are staying at a house near here for the holidays," Ravi answered.

"Which house?" Raphael asked, shaken.

"There is a house just up the hill about two miles from here. Alister bought it recently," Ravi replied.

"He bought that house? Ravi, how did he find that?" Raphael questioned.

"I saw it on your computer as a listing. I thought it was cool, and Alister likes places like that. We always send each other stuff like that, so I thought he would like to see it. I didn't think he would have bought it!" Ravi responded.

Raphael grabbed Ravi's jacket and worriedly said, "Son, tell me those kids aren't there. Tell me that's not true."

"What the hell is happening, dad? What was that thing, and why do you have a gun on you? Didn't you say you were going on a business trip?" Ravi asked.

Raphael sighed deeply; the sorrow in his eyes could be read easily. "Ravi, I want you to listen to me. This isn't the life I want for you. Don't ask anything further. As your father, I refuse to do what my great-grandfather did to me. Please, son, I may not be your blood, but you are my boy. Listen to me. I want you to never look back on this when this is over. Right now, we have to go to the house; your cousins are in real danger. True evil is lurking in this mountain," Raphael explained.

"You can't ask me to do that. I want to know what we are up against here, especially if our family is in danger. Please, dad," Ravi pleaded.

Raphael looked at him and recognized the determination in his eyes. It reminded him of his great-grandfather. He thought to himself, *He doesn't need to know what's out there. I can protect his innocence. I will not allow you into this life, my child.* "Alright, son, I'll level with you. What you saw was a demon, or as close to one as it gets," Raphael informed him.

"A what?" asked Ravi. Adelheid held his hand.

"Most of these things are folktales parents tell their kids to keep them from misbehaving. But some of them have very real origins. This one, in particular, stems from Krampus," said Raphael.

"Krampus? You mean like evil Santa Claus?" asked Ravi.

"Precisely! But it's not exactly linked to the jolly old man. Krampus existed long before stories of Santa Claus emerged. In fact, they held festivals for him; they made offerings and gave human sacrifices to appease the creature. Over the years, the story of Santa Claus overshadowed the once God. Now, it's starving and hungry. Every few years, it comes out during the winter solstice to feast. And while it's here, it drags believers in Santa Claus to the afterlife, young and old," Raphael continued to explain.

"Oh my God," Adelheid gasped.

"My great-grandfather tried hunting this thing when he was about your age. He was obsessed with ending its terror. He passed his knowledge down to my father, who passed it on to me. And now, after all this time, it's finally woken up to eat. Once we end this, our family can rest, and there will be no more darkness in the world like this," Raphael finished.

"Alright, dad. I am all ears; how do we kill this

thing? I wanna help," said Ravi.

"First, we need to get back to your cousins, son. If the Yule Goat shows itself, it could be too late to save them," Raphael answered.

"The Yule Goat?" Ravi enquired.

"It's Krampus' death omen, a manifestation of the creature itself. If the goat reveals itself to you, death will follow before the break of dawn," Raphael replied.

"Um, dad, by chance, would that goat be over five feet tall when on all fours?" Ravi's asked shakily.

Raphael's eyes began to tear up; his lips twitched and turned into a frown. "Son, tell me you didn't see it!"

"James and I saw it earlier in the woods," Ravi uttered.

"No...," Raphael's voice broke.

CHAPTER

10

Alister and James were the only ones still awake in the house; the kids had tired themselves out from singing Christmas carols and crashed from the sugar of the hot chocolates they were given. James listened to their childhood Christmas songs and reminisced while Alister was on the tablet surfing the internet. James noticed that Alister had worn a serious expression on his face ever since they sat down with the kids. It was unlike him since he loved singing and being part of the noise too.

James was worried about what had him this quiet.

KRAMPUS

He doesn't get like this unless he's planning something. What's going on in his head? It's not common to see him this serious, especially on Christmas, James thought. "Everything ok, man?" James whispered softly so as not to wake the kids.

Alister looked up at him and used his index finger to beckon James into the kitchen. Alister entered the kitchen first, followed by James. Opening the fridge, he took out two beers and handed one to James.

"What's up with you? You seem off," said James.

"We had a really big scare earlier. I saw things, you saw things, and I can't shake this feeling of dread ever since we got here," Alister answered.

"What about it?" questioned James.

"I did some digging and couldn't find anything based on what either of us saw. But then I remembered the ornament I'd stepped on; the note inside is from that Christmas song, 'He sees you when you're sleeping.' I thought about it and decided to look into all things Christmas, especially the origins of that song. Santa Claus was always said to have a shadow side, a wicked, evil sidekick called Krampus.

"I thought those were just stories. I mean, we

have seen movies about it, and it's all about this anti-Christmas creature coming for the kids who were on the naughty list. But those stories weren't always the true portrayal of what Krampus is. Each version of him hails from a different region: Certa, Perchten, Black Peter, Belsnickle, and Klaubauf. All of these places have different versions of the story," Alister explained as he handed James the tablet to scroll through each version of the stories he had read.

Alister took a sip of beer and looked over at the kids. He turned back to James and continued, "I dug a little deeper. It turns out that the original lore for Krampus stemmed from pre-German paganism. Krampus comes from the word Krampen which means 'claw,' and the lore states that he comes from the Alps."

James' attention moved from the tablet to Alister, "The Alps? As in, where we are right now?"

"Yeah, and this also matches the hands we both saw. They mentioned what it looked like: a long bony hand with claws wrapped in chains. It carries the bones of the people he feasted on and is covered in a thick black cloak, stained with the blood of those it killed," Alister responded.

"You really think that's real? I mean, come on… I know what I saw, but this is too much," James exclaimed.

"I don't know. I really don't," Alister replied.

"Though I mean, it's all here: from the chains to the hand. They even mentioned the goat," James stated.

Alister quickly looked at him and asked, "The goat? What goat?"

James took out his phone and opened the chat where Ravi had shared the picture. Alister looked at the photo and brightened the phone screen to the max. He zoomed in on the goat behind them, standing almost as tall as they were. Ravi's downward angle showed the goat with its head on the ground gnawing at something. Alister zoomed in further and saw someone's hand on the ground and blood spattered on the grass.

"James…," Alister muttered, showing him the phone. James' eyes widened when he looked at the zoomed-in picture.

"Oh my God… It's not the goat that was smelling; it was the remains of that person!" James exclaimed.

"Not that, James. Look closer. Look at the

bracelet on that person's hand. Doesn't it look familiar?" asked Alister.

"Holy crap. It looks like Ravi's keychain," James replied.

Just then, Alister looked over to the kids and saw Krampus standing and holding Alyssa in the air with its mouth wide open. Alister's breathing locked up. Seeing Alister like this, James immediately turned to the living room and screamed out Alyssa's name when he saw what was happening. Krampus dropped her on the floor and swiftly snuck up the chimney, howling as it did and waking the rest of the kids. Frightened by the sound it had made, Benji and Shay grabbed onto each other and called out to their uncles.

Alister ran to Alyssa, lying lifeless on the ground. Her eyes were white and rolled back into her head. "Alyssa, wake up, doll. Come on, wake up," he called out to her.

James went to Benji and Shay and embraced them tightly, turning them away from Alyssa and Alister.

"Come on, baby girl, wake up," Alister pleaded as he lightly tapped her on her cheek several times.

Tears welled in his eyes as he cried out, "Wake up!" As Alyssa's skin turned pale, he covered his mouth to hold back his screams.

Hearing Alister's heartbreaking call to his niece, James let go of Benji and Shay and sat beside Alister, who was holding her. He placed his finger on Alyssa's neck and placed his ear on her chest. "She's still alive. She's breathing, and her heart is pumping normally," James informed Alister.

"Then why won't she wake up?" asked Alister.

James took her in his arms and said, "Alyssa, baby, can you hear me?"

"Alister!" Ravi called out from outside the house. Alister got up, ran to the door, and unlocked it. Ravi, Adelheid, and Raphael stood on the porch. The trio was shocked by Alister's distressed state.

"Bro, you ok?" Ravi asked.

Raphael walked up to him. "Alister?" he said with a worried look.

Alister couldn't find the words to speak. He stood there while his breathing grew out of control. Raphael slapped him. "Pull yourself together, son. Focus on me. What happened?" Raphael asked.

"Alyssa... She won't wake up," Alister muttered as he turned and looked at James crouched on the ground with an unconscious Alyssa in his hands.

"Ravi, go inside with Heidi," Raphael ordered. Stepping inside with Alister, he shut the door behind Ravi and Heidi and took Alister in his arms. "It's ok, son. It's ok. We need you to keep it together," said Raphael, comforting Alister.

"She won't wake up," Alister repeated, his voice cracking.

"Shhh," Raphael held Alister tighter. "It's alright, son. It's ok; come on, she needs her uncle to be strong for her right now. Wipe those tears, and let's go fix this!"

Alister took a minute to compose himself before he walked into the living room and joined everyone huddled around James.

"She's not waking up, but her heartbeat and her breathing are ok," James informed Raphael.

"What happened to her?" Ravi asked his stepdad.

Raphael was hesitant to answer. He looked around at the kids, Alister and James, not wanting to reveal what was really happening.

"Krampus took her soul, is what happened!" Alister stated. All eyes averted to him. Shocked, Raphael exchanged looks with Ravi.

"Did you tell him anything?" Raphael questioned Ravi.

"Tell me what?" asked Alister.

James chimed in, "Yeah, tell him what?" as he looked at Ravi and Raphael.

"Alister, what do you know about Krampus?" asked Raphael.

"Answer my question first, Uncle Raph. What did you mean just now?" Alister pressed.

"Heidi, can you take the kids into the kitchen and fix them something warm while I talk to my boys?" Raphael requested.

"Of course," Adelheid replied as she took Benji and Shay by the hand and marched to the kitchen.

Raphael turned back to Alister and James. "You saw it?" he mumbled.

"Yeah, we did," James responded.

"Did the kids see it?" Raphael probed.

"No, Benji and Shay were asleep. They woke up when it ran off, right after it did this to Alyssa," Alister answered.

"Was its mouth open? Did you see the light in its eyes?" Raphael questioned.

"I don't know. I didn't really notice the eyes, but the mouth was open. It held her up in the air like it was about to swallow her whole," Alister replied.

"No, thankfully, it wasn't going to eat her. If it was, she would be dead already. I don't know if this is better or worse, but what it really did was take her soul," Raphael explained.

"Excuse me?" James stated.

"He's right; Krampus feeds on human flesh, but he takes the souls of those who lost their faith in the spirit of the winter solstice festival. Every single one of us is on that list because it's an old tradition and not one from where we grew up," Alister clarified.

"That's right; that means every one of us is on the chopping block here. Son, where did you learn all of this?" asked Raphael.

"I did some research," answered Alister.

"That is some research! These things date back to the twelfth century," Raphael exclaimed.

"Well, I'm good at this stuff. It comes with the

turf of being a writer," Alister replied.

"Boys, I love you all dearly, and I don't want this life for you. I wish to God that you hadn't come here and seen the things you've seen. I really do. But I also raised you like my own kids; I know you won't let this one go, either. Krampus is the embodiment of real evil, and tonight, you boys are going to help me stop it," Raphael declared.

"What? And leave me behind? I don't think so," Adelheid quipped, standing behind them.

"Heidi...," Ravi mumbled.

"No, I don't want that protective boyfriend speech," Adelheid ranted.

"Boyfriend?" said James, looking over at Ravi.

"Oh, don't even start," Ravi replied, blushing and turning away from James.

"I am a part of this too. Like it or not," Adelheid responded.

"She's right; once Krampus comes for you, he will not leave without you unless you offer him another in your place. This stems from the ancient rituals and sacrifices they performed back in the day. Believe it or not, Krampus isn't really evil; it wants children to be joyful during the winter solstice. There was a celebration where parents used to whip kids who misbehaved during the festival with the branches of birch trees. It marked them for Krampus and was the first step of prepping them for being the sacrifice," Raphael explained.

"That's cruel," Alister exclaimed.

"Those were different times; people used to line up to be sacrificed back then. It was deemed the highest form of worship for the creature at the time. Now, it's been twisted into a monster story. Their efforts to overshadow it with Christmas replacing the winter solstice and Santa Claus replacing Krampus is exactly what created the creature of the Yuletide you met today. I saw your firewood basket outside; the birch trees are what led it here. When you burnt the branches, the smoke marked each of you. Now you're being hunted; whether it wants to eat you or condemn your soul is the real question," said Raphael.

"Then, how do we stop it? Can we even do anything to this Krampus creature?" asked James.

"Yes, with the evergreen trees built into the Christmas festival. Evergreen trees ward off the creature, and when decorated with Christmas lights, the beast thinks it's on fire, which is why most people have never seen this creature. Every house on the block has a Christmas tree in their home. Real or fake, it tricks the beast and keeps it away. They didn't specifically state this in what I've read. But if they put the lights to trick it into thinking the tree was on fire, I think the only thing that could harm Krampus is a burning evergreen stake," Alister deduced.

"You learned all that and pieced together exactly what you'd need in one night – something that took my great-grandfather and me decades to figure out! But Alister is right; a burning evergreen stake can kill a Krampus, but it's also what can ward it off. In your fireplace, replace all the wood you have with evergreen tree logs. The smoke it creates will keep Krampus from coming into the house," said Raphael.

"We only gathered birch; we didn't get that far into the woods to get any evergreen," Ravi informed him.

"That's alright. I have an entire trunk filled with logs. Come on, boys, help me bring it inside," Raphael responded as he stood up. Alister, Ravi, and James followed him outside. Quickly pulling Raphael's SUV into the garage and offloading the wood, there was barely enough room to snugly fit the vehicle in the garage.

Once all the wood was loaded inside, Alister and James stoked the new fire until it was blazing hot. The fog and the cold weather around the house dropped slightly. Hearing a howl rip through the air, everyone stood still until the sound faded. "This will only make it mad, but it will be safe here. Nobody steps foot outside that door, hear me? And keep the kids close to the fire," said Raphael as he raised a piece of evergreen branch and began to carve stakes for the five of them.

"What about Alyssa? Is she going to be ok?" asked Alister.

"She will stay in that coma indefinitely until this thing is dead. Or it will hold onto her soul and drag it to hell with it," Raphael answered.

"Dad… Is that why your mom has been in a coma all these years?" Ravi enquired.

Raphael paused for a moment. Looking at Ravi, he nodded at him. James and Alister bowed their heads in sorrow, and Adelheid covered her mouth and gasped.

"How long?" asked Ravi.

"When she was fourteen... She had just had me. I was a couple months old. My great-grandfather told me about it when I was just a little boy. He was hellbent on killing the creature that took his grandchild from him and my mother from me. I'm so sorry you boys got caught up in all of this. Had I not been driven by revenge, I might have covered my tracks better. Then Ravi would never have found this house on my computer. Alister never would have bought it, and Alyssa would be sipping hot chocolate with her cousins as we speak. I'm sorry I let you boys down. I tried my best to protect you from this life," Raphael declared.

The house stood still. Alister and the others sat speechless as Raphael's eyes welled up.

CHAPTER

11

Raphael and Ravi finished making the last of the evergreen stakes. Alister buried himself in research looking through every bit of lore he could find about Krampus. James and Adelheid made sure the fire kept burning hot while they sat with a knife and scraped an evergreen log, extracting sawdust. Raphael and Ravi entered the living room and sat beside James and Adelheid. "This is really good; let me show you guys what we are doing with this," Raphael said as he walked over to his backpack and retrieved a tray with a mold that contained several holes.

He scooped the sawdust into the molds evenly and packed them in. Sealing off the end, he flipped the mold over, and out came shotgun shells loaded with the sawdust.

"Sawdust rounds?" asked James.

"Mixed in with some splinters. When the shells fire, the dust ignites, along with the splinters. It can hurt the creature, but unfortunately, it's not fatal to the beast. Still, it's a good option to repel it for a bit," said Raphael. "But not just any ingredients will work. There is one special step we must do before any of this works." Raphael placed the stakes and the bullets on the floor and chanted, 'Exorcizamus te, omnis immundus spiritus. Omnis Satanica potestas, omnis incursio infernalis adversii. Omnis congregatio et secta diabolica, ergo, draco maledicte ecclesiam tuam. Secura tibi facias libertate servire, te rogamus, audi nos.'

"This is the oldest Latin incantation of protection known to man. It will dispel any evil from around you, but most importantly, it purifies. In this case, objects, but this purity is also fatal to these creatures," Raphael explained.

"I started chanting that when Krampus came for Heidi. You always told me it would destroy the evil around me. So, my first instinct was to start saying it, but all it did was make it mad and attack me," Ravi mentioned.

"That's my boy! Yes, this prayer does work, but it won't be fatal to Krampus; it will only exasperate it at best. That's probably why it attacked you like that instead of eating you on the spot. It wanted to stop the chanting. But these bullets, this will do way more damage," Raphael explained.

"Is that what you shot it with back in Wengen?" Ravi asked.

"That's right," answered Raphael.

"Why didn't you kill it with an evergreen stake back then?" Ravi enquired.

Raphael bowed his head briefly, "I was too far away to use the stake. But even if I did, I couldn't have killed it. It wasn't going to steal your soul; it was going to devour you. I wouldn't have made it in time to kill it without it killing you first. I won't lose my boy, too," said Raphael.

"What do you mean you couldn't? You have the

weapon to kill it, don't you?" James asked.

"He did, but it's not that simple," Adelheid responded. Raphael looked over at her with a sad expression.

"I don't understand," Ravi stated.

"I think I can shine some light on that. Raphael couldn't kill Krampus because just hitting it with the stake won't do any good," Alister explained as he walked over with the tablet. "Krampus is only vulnerable when it takes souls. Did I get that right, Uncle Raph?"

"That's right, son. Krampus is vulnerable when the lights go dark in its eyes. In order to take the souls, it must bare its own when feeding on someone else's life. Once that link is made, killing it during that time will end it for good," Raphael explained.

Ravi thought about that for a moment before saying, "Wait a second. Something doesn't add up; if you can't kill that thing unless it's taking a soul, how were you intending on finishing it?" Ravi looked at his stepdad. Adelheid watched on as Ravi and Raphael exchanged piercing glares.

"No... Don't tell me you were using Heidi as

bait!" Ravi shouted as he stood up, enraged.

"Ravi!" Adelheid called out to him.

"Tell me you weren't going to use her as bait for that thing, dad!" Ravi belted.

"I had no choice, Ravi," Raphael declared.

"Bullshit, don't tell me you didn't!" Ravi shouted. Shay and Benji were startled by his outburst. Alister got in Ravi's face quickly.

"Yoo, not in front of the kids. What the hell is the matter with you?" Alister whispered harshly as he grabbed Ravi's arm.

Ravi pulled his arm away and shoved Alister back. "Get the fuck off me!" Ravi shouted.

"Hey!" Alister called out. Running to him, he grabbed him by the jacket and pushed him against the wall. "Watch your mouth; there are kids here!" Ravi broke Alister's grip and reversed it, throwing Alister into the wall and trading places with him.

"How would you feel if he used someone you loved as bait, huh!? What if he had used the kids as bait and left them alone?" asked Ravi.

James rushed between them and easily forced them apart. Turning to Ravi, James pointed to his face and sternly said, "Calm yourself."

Ravi slapped away his hand and tried to shove James out of the way. James pushed him back and sent Ravi stumbling into the wall. Raphael grabbed him when he tried to rush James again. "Ravi, calm down," he said.

"How could you do that? You weren't even there; you weren't even there in time to kill it from attacking me. What would have happened to her had I not been there when I was? Tell me what would have happened if I didn't go looking for her!?" Ravi shouted while looking back at Raphael, holding him.

Raphael let go of his grip; Ravi stepped away and turned to him. "How could you use her as bait like that?" Ravi raged.

"It wasn't his choice," Adelheid said. Ravi turned to her. Alister noticed she had the same charm as Ravi on her wrist.

"You offered yourself as bait?" Ravi asked shakily.

"Ravi, you and your dad have been a long-time family friend. I am the reason he came out here in the first place. I know I told you my parents were not home, but I failed to mention some more details about that," Adelheid stated.

James looked at Alister. "No way... Could it be them?" James muttered.

"I think so," Alister replied.

"What? Am I missing something here?" said Ravi.

"Ravi, my mother was attacked by Krampus a few weeks ago. She's in a coma, too, like your niece," Adelheid explained.

"Her dad and I tried to kill it. We spent day in, day out, exhausting every plan we came up with, but without bait, we had no chance. Her dad offered himself as bait, and he was eaten alive. It happened so fast that I couldn't have done anything to save him. When Krampus feeds, he's like a rabid beast. He's hungry and starving and will gobble you up in the blink of an eye.

"When it takes souls, it stalks the prey. It's a slow process; it would freeze the land and blind you in darkness. When it hunts, it isolates you before striking. I was about to get Heidi out of there when it returned for her. We knew he wanted her soul," Raphael explained.

"And I was game. This was my choice. Do you understand me?" Adelheid asked Ravi.

"But, Heidi...," Ravi began.

"But nothing. I would do anything for my family. I would give anything to get my mom back, even if it meant I traded places with her. Wouldn't you do it for your family?" questioned Adelheid.

Ravi turned to Alister and James. He calmed himself by taking a few deep breaths. "In a heartbeat," he replied.

"We all would," Alister chimed in.

"What did you boys mean when you said, 'Could it be them?' a moment ago?" said Raphael.

"Ravi and I took a picture with the goat in the woods. Remember when we smelt something really foul, Ravi?" James asked.

"Yeah, I do," Ravi responded.

"If you zoom in on the picture with the brightness all the way up, you can see it was eating the remains of a corpse on the ground," James explained.

"And on the arm, there was a charm like the one you wear on the keychain. I just noticed Heidi also had one. So, we figured it might have been her dad from what was said just now," Alister finished.

"Boys, what you saw is called the Yule Goat. It's a death omen that follows Krampus. Seeing it means you are marked for death by the night's end, " Raphael stated. "Ravi and James, you boys need to sit this one out. Let me, Heidi and Alister take the reins on this."

"You can't be serious?" Ravi exclaimed.

"I am deadly serious, son; I will not lose either of you boys tonight. Am I clear? All we need to do is make it to tomorrow," Raphael declared.

"Alright, Uncle Raph. How are we going to do this?" asked James.

"I might have an idea—" said Alister as he looked towards them.

CHAPTER

12

Midnight struck, and the darkness of the night had reached its apex. Alister gathered everyone to pitch his plan to kill the creature. "Alright, everyone, this is what I have in mind. Krampus is hungry; it's starving after all those years, right? That means it's guaranteed to show if we dangle some food in front of it. This is still just a creature; it's acting on instinct. We can outsmart this thing if that's the case. I still don't like using Heidi as bait, but it's all we have. Are you sure you're up for this?" Alister looked at Adelheid as he asked this.

CREATURE OF THE YULETIDE

"I'm sure," Adelheid responded as she held Ravi's hand and smiled subtly. Ravi bore a worried expression.

"Alright, we're sure as hell not bringing that thing inside, which means we are gonna go out there. Inside this house is the safest place for the kids and for Ravi and James. Krampus can't get to either of you as long as that evergreen fire is burning," Alister began.

"It might be a creature, but it's not stupid, son. It won't come to her if we are there. Outside is nothing but an open field, and I don't think you're crazy enough to go into those woods. The reason I took so long to get to Heidi back at Wengen is that I needed to be away from her. It won't show if there is a threat nearby. We can't exactly stand close to her and wait for it to show its face," Raphael exclaimed.

"Oh, that's exactly what we're going to do," said Alister.

"How? Listen, man, I don't mean to be a buzzkill, but I've seen this thing. It takes seconds to do what it needs to do. Everything happened in a split second. Do you know how close you would need to be to get to it in time?" Ravi questioned.

"Yeah, we've seen it first-hand, too, when it took Alyssa. We were about ten, maybe fifteen feet away, but it took off in no time. You need to be within arm's reach of her. There's no way you can stay that close and hide at the same time," said James.

"What if it couldn't see us?" Alister remarked.

"How? Where are you going to hide? It's nothing but grass out there. The only place you can possibly hide is if this went down in the woods, and we've already established that's a no-go," Raphael said.

"It's a theory, but I think this will work. You said Christmas trees were put into homes to keep Krampus away, correct? The lights trick it into thinking the tree is on fire. Maybe I'm crazy, but I'm taking a shot in the dark and saying its eyesight is messed up. We brought a Christmas tree for the holidays, and the last owners have one too. What if we set up both of them on either side of Heidi? We could hide behind it until it's go-time. Once those eyes go dark, we just need to swing; no room for error," Alister explained.

"I don't know, guys. We don't know for sure if that'll work," Ravi stated.

"Alister is on to something. The family that lived

here had a tree, but Krampus still reached its hand through the fireplace, grabbed a child, and ate it," said Raphael.

"Oh my God," Alister exclaimed.

"That's why they left everything and ran from this place," James mused.

"Now it makes sense why this place was so cheap. They would have given it away for free. They took whatever they got, ran with it, and left all this behind," said Alister.

"When Heidi told me about what was happening, I contacted the family that lived here. I scoped this place out the moment I got here," said Raphael.

"How long did the last owners live here?" asked Alister.

"An old gentleman bought the place about four years ago. Why do you ask?" Raphael questioned.

"They had journals: a log of stuff that occurred over the last four years. I swept cover to cover of those books. How could they not know about this?" Alister wondered.

"Krampus is too weak to show every year. Thanks to the effort to make Christmas a mainstream holiday and with Santa Claus overshadowing the existence of Krampus, there were no more offerings and sacrifices. It's what made the creature into what it is today. It's hungry and trying to survive. The winter solstice ended on the 21st of December, but it's still here because it's still hungry. But I have my own theory of that," Raphael answered. "I think it needs more souls, more food. The lore states that once it marks you, it won't leave until it has your soul."

"Heidi was its last marked soul," said James.

"That means it's backed into a corner here. It has to come for her, even if Heidi is in the middle of two lit Christmas trees. I've got the backup power that can run those lights for hours, long enough to wait out the night. I say that's our best shot," Alister declared as he looked at everyone around the room.

One by one, they each agreed to the plan. "Alright then, let's go hunting!" Raphael announced.

CHAPTER

13

Raphael and Alister swept the house to ensure there was no sign of Krampus outside. James and Ravi prepared the trees for the plan. Alister followed Raphael into the room furthest from the living room. He looked around and, seeing no one else nearby, closed the door behind them. Raphael moved the phone away from his ear, turned to Alister, and said, "Son?"

"We need to talk," said Alister.

"What's this about?" asked Raphael curiously.

"The death omen — Ravi and James saw the Yule Goat," said Alister.

Raphael looked away and leaned against a wall, "So, you read about that too, huh?"

"You know, keeping them away from Krampus will do no good. When the goat shows itself, it's a demand for presents. Those who refuse the Yule Goat will die, and their souls will be dragged to hell, chained to Krampus' sleigh that the beast tows," Alister remarked.

"That's right, which is why we need to end this tonight. The Yule Goat will come on Christmas eve; if we don't finish this before then, Ravi and James are as good as dead. Unlike Krampus, the Goat isn't a physical creature. It's a manifestation of Krampus. The firewood we burn will do nothing to keep it out. Maybe we can repel it, but I can't say for sure. It's merely a manifestation of Krampus; over the years, its will became a weapon to enter the houses of people it demanded offerings from. Our stakes and the smoke from the fire will do nothing. Ravi and James will be ripped apart and dragged out of the house, bloody and screaming, by a creature we can't see or touch," Raphael clarified.

"But what does it want? What can we offer it so

that it doesn't take them?" Alister enquired.

"A life," Raphael responded as he looked at Alister. "A life offered is worth more than a life taken. Krampus can kill and eat endlessly and still not be satisfied. The reason it's starving isn't that it hasn't eaten; it's because no offerings have been made to appease the beast. Only willing participants will appease the beast, which is why people lined up to offer themselves in the old days. Presenting someone against their will would only anger the beast," Raphael explained.

"So, if it gets a willing sacrifice, it will leave, right?" asked Alister.

"It would," Raphael answered.

"Then offer me in their place," said Alister. "I'll happily do it."

Raphael leaned off the wall and walked to Alister. "What did you say?" he snarled.

"Offer me when the Yule Goat comes," Alister repeated.

Raphael grabbed Alister by his jacket collar and jerked him. "Like hell I will!" Raphael cried out.

"Think of everyone downstairs right now. If we

fail, we stand to lose Heidi, James, and Ravi at the very least, as opposed to me alone. We won't endanger Heidi, and I can save my cousins. It's a good deal," Alister stated.

"It's a stupid deal. I will not trade one of my boys to save the others, nor will I let them die. That's the last time you speak of this, son. Am I clear," asked Raphael.

"You're gambling lives out there. We are about to set off a trap that 'might' work, using an innocent girl as bait who 'might' survive. And that's 'if' we get the timing right. Worst of all, if we miss our shot, she will die, and the rest of us will be next. And even if we manage to escape after messing up, Ravi and James will be the next to go indefinitely. This plan is standing on a major 'if.' At least if you offer me up, we know for sure Ravi and James will be safe, and Krampus will leave. This way, my life would have been worth something," Alister declared.

"What!? And your life didn't mean something before? Do you think that low of yourself that you would run away from your life and now give it up? Do you believe you are worth this little to the people around you? Have you that grim an opinion of yourself, son?" Raphael tightened his grip as his voice shook, his face burdened with sorrow.

"I'm not going to let them die out there, Uncle Raph. I couldn't live with myself if anything happened to them. I don't think I would come back from that kind of pain. I would gladly trade my life for theirs," said Alister.

"And how do you think your family would feel if you died? Do you think they would recover from it? I watched you boys run around in diapers, playing pirates and witches and ghost hunting in the house at night. You are the spark that lights that fire in them. You are like a big brother to those boys. You're a hero to your nieces and nephews. And you may not be my blood, but you are my boy. I won't let any of you die here tonight. I promise," Raphael responded, tears filling his eyes. Raphael embraced Alister.

Suddenly, the sound of chains clattering in the distance could be heard. A loud thump on the ceiling shook the house, and the howl of the beast echoed in the darkness outside.

"It's after midnight; it's Christmas eve—" Alister said as he looked at his watch.

CHAPTER

14

Alister and Raphael hurried downstairs. Ravi and the others had just finished wrapping the Christmas tree with lights and connecting it to the power backups. "We're all set. Are you guys ready?" asked Ravi.

"No, but here goes nothing," said Adelheid.

"Guys, why can't we just jump into Uncle Raph's SUV and haul ass out of here?" James enquired.

"We won't make it far. Out there, we are sitting ducks. The cold weather would freeze the engine in minutes, and the wheels and everything else would seize up. Krampus is isolating us here; nothing gets in or out. We have to do this right here," Alister said as he grabbed one of the trees.

"Heidi, let's go," said Raphael, strapping the shotgun to his back. On the side of the gun were six extra shells. Raphael dug into his bag, pulled out two lighters, and stuffed them in his pocket before hurrying outside.

James and Ravi grabbed onto Alister before he walked away. "Don't let my girl die, or I'll kill you myself," said Ravi.

"Don't I always have your back?" Alister smirked. James and Ravi tapped him on the shoulder and nodded at him. Alister returned the gesture.

Alister and Raphael each held a six-foot tree in front of them and walked outside, setting it on the ground so they could conceal themselves behind it, Adelheid hesitantly stood between the trees; the blinking lights of the trees shone on her. Alister and Raphael each held a stake in hand at the ready. Ravi and James kept the kids away from them, huddling together at the other end of the house. The sound of chains rattling in the night sky was now closer. Falling onto the ground, it kicked up a large dust cloud.

KRAMPUS

Krampus rose from a crouched position, its skull head and beak-like mouth peeking out of the hooded cloak over its head.

Bones tethered to the cloak of the beast jingled in the winds. Chains dragged on the ground, wrapping around the beast as it cautiously marched towards Adelheid. Alister and Raphael gripped the stakes tightly. Ravi and James prepared them beforehand: lighter fluid was dripping off the tips of the stakes. Raphael took out a lighter and tossed it to Alister. Sparking a flame, he waited to light the stake to end the beast. Krampus unleashed a deep bloodcurdling growl. Adelheid shook in fear as the beast's jaw unhinged and hung low. Opening its mouth large enough to swallow her whole, she could see a black ooze-like substance holding the skeletal jaw to the beast's skull. It unleashed a fearsome howl into the night. Adelheid screamed in fear, her body frozen in terror. Ravi got up and ran to the door.

"Ravi, don't!" James screamed.

Ravi stopped dead in his tracks when he heard the sound of heavy hooves stomping on the floor ahead of him. Each stomp on the floor cracked it more and more until the imprint of the large hooves was seen etched into the floor. A cloud of black smoke rose from the floor and moved closer to Ravi as he stepped back. The smoke thickened, and the silhouette of the Yule Goat could be seen as the smoke wrapped around its invisible body. Two luminous eyes opened and glared at them, only visible through the smoke.

James grabbed the flashlight and shone it on the creature, illuminating the living room, its beams reaching outside. The light of the flashlight startled Alister. He turned to the window and saw the shadow of the Yule Goat inside, pushing off and raising up to stand on its hind legs, extending long bony hands toward Ravi.

"No…," Alister muttered.

"Alister, now!" Raphael yelled.

Alister turned around and saw Krampus' eyes had gone dark while holding Adelheid in his hand. He rushed out from behind the tree and drove the stake into the side of the beast.

"Nooo!!! You didn't light the stake!" Raphael shrieked as he charged in with a lit evergreen stake. Krampus' eyes lit up once more. Dropping Adelheid to the ground, Alister dove and caught her. Raphael thrusted the stake towards the beast. As it raised its hand to block the attack, the stake pierced through, and the beast roared in pain. Raphael pulled the shotgun off his back and unloaded two shots on the beast, causing it to flail around and howl in agony. Krampus jumped back and vanished into the air.

James backed the kids into a corner behind him as Ravi slowly inched away from the Yule Goat's extended hands.

"Get down, son!" Raphael screamed, aiming the shotgun after reloading two more rounds in it. Ravi ducked down quickly, and James turned and shielded the kids. Raphael opened fire on the Yule Goat. Both shots appeared to connect, smoking and burning at the point of impact. The smoke quickly dissipated into the ground. Alister and Adelheid hurried back inside and grabbed more stakes.

"There isn't much time; that won't do anything to it. Listen to me...," Raphael paused and threw the shotgun to Ravi. "I love you all. Boys, be good to each other."

Ravi looked at his stepdad, bewildered. Alister

quickly turned around and yelled, "Uncle Raph, no!"

Raphael walked outside and dropped to his knees. "I offer myself!" Raphael yelled into the darkness.

"NO!!!!!" Alister screamed and rushed over to him. As Ravi ran to the door, Raphael was impaled by the antler-like horns of the Yule Goat. The beast stood up on its hind legs, with Raphael suspended by its horns. The Yule Goat whipped its head to the side, flinging Raphael off its horns, and sent him tumbling down the hill.

"It didn't take the offering," Alister whispered.

Ravi bawled in pain, calling Raphael's name in vain as he watched the lifeless body tumble down the hill. Alister forcefully pulled him inside and closed the door. Ravi fought to run to his stepdad but was held back by Alister. James and Adelheid quickly came to Alister's aid to hold Ravi back, kicking and screaming as he tried to get to Raphael.

The house shook as Krampus growled once more. Shay began to cry at the sound of the dreadful noise surrounding the house. Benji hugged her and covered her eyes. The trio managed to drag Ravi to the living room, and Alister slapped him to get his attention.

"Ravi! Listen! Listen, this is all my fault, but I am going to fix this," said Alister frantically.

"What are you talking about?!" James and Heidi asked.

"Listen, your dad offered himself in place of you and James. The death omen of the Yule Goat will kill you both, and we couldn't stop it. So, your dad offered himself as a sacrifice in your place. It didn't work because he didn't want to be sacrificed, but he did it anyway because he felt he had to," Alister replied quickly.

"What the hell are you talking about?" Ravi frantically asked.

"Listen to me; don't I always have your backs? Trust me on this," Alister responded.

"Are you crazy? Absolutely not! You're not giving up yourself!" said James.

"I'm the oldest; it's my job to keep you safe! I wasn't strong enough to kill this thing, but I can do this! I will trade my life to protect my cousins, end of the discussion," said Alister. James and Ravi grabbed him and held him back from leaving.

"Please let me do this," Alister said calmly, looking away from them as his hands shook.

"We already lost you once. Don't do this to us again," said James.

The sound of the door opening diverted their attention. Everyone's heart skipped a beat when they saw Benji standing by the door, looking back at them.

"Don't worry, Uncle Alister. Benji is strong; he can protect his cousins," said Benji.

"Benji, noooo!!!!!" Alister screamed as he and the others ran full sprint to Benji.

Benji turned to the darkness and yelled, "Take me instead!"

"NOOOO!!!!!" Alister and the others cried out.

They heard the sound of chains rattling fiercely. In the blink of an eye, Benji was snatched from the door. Alister, James, and Ravi dove with extended hands to grab Benji, narrowly missing him before he was snatched. Krampus took off running into the woods, howling into the night. Benji's scream grew fainter the further he got.

"Benji!!!" Alister screamed, chasing after the

creature of the Yuletide, its hooves stomping ahead of him and howling into the night. Benji cried out for his uncles. Alister, James, Ravi, and Adelheid chased Krampus through the woods.

***

Shay was left alone with Alyssa's body at the house in the heat of the moment. Sitting with her cousin near the fire, she kept her warm. Suddenly, the sound of hooves approached from behind. The three-year-old turned around and saw the beast coming towards her, the light of its eyes shining on her plump rosy cheeks.

Lifting its hoof from the ground, the smoke formed into a long bony hand resembling Krampus' hand. Shay reached out to the shadowy hand.

***

Alister ran ahead of the others and almost caught up to the beast. Benji reached out and pleaded for his uncle to save him. Just as Alister was practically close enough to grab Benji's hand, Krampus leaped into the air. He jumped well over fifteen feet into the air, using the trees as a foothold, and moved by jumping from tree to tree. Alister stumbled when he attempted to jump and grab Benji, tumbling to the ground. Ravi and James ran past him, but Heidi stopped to help Alister to his feet. Quickly getting his footing, Alister managed to catch up to Ravi and James. He and James held a stake in hand while Ravi, with the shotgun, reloaded as he ran.

Up ahead, Krampus landed on an old iron sleigh at the edge of the mountain. Zooming beside the trio was the Yule Goat galloping at full speed when James noticed Shay was hanging from its mouth.

"Shay!!!!!" James screamed.

The Yule Goat tossed Shay to Krampus along with a chain tied to its neck. The child fell into the sleigh, screaming beside Benji. Ravi took two shots at Krampus, causing the dark cloak to burn. Krampus turned to them and growled. The power of its bellowing vibrations rattled the leaves of the trees as the trio made it out into the clearing on the cliff's edge. Shay, in a panic, tried to climb out of the sleigh, her head and arms reaching over the edge. The Yule Goat ran off the mountain's edge and pulled the sleigh into the air.

"Ravi, shoot the stake!" Alister screamed. Ravi quickly did as instructed. The lighter fluid ignited. Alister ran up and threw the stake at Krampus, piercing its shoulder. The sleigh took off at speed, and Benji and Shay screamed for help as they disappeared into the night sky. Alister, Ravi, and James stood helplessly and watched on as their little cries faded into the darkness.

Alister collapsed to his knees, breathing heavily. Adelheid ran to Ravi screaming, and James looked up into the sky, frozen in fear.

"It took them—" Alister whispered. "It should have been me…." His tears hit the ground below. The dark clouds parted and revealed the night sky, with Krampus now gone. The temperature also returned to normal, and the fog disappeared. "I promised I wouldn't leave them alone again…."

CHAPTER

15

On their way back home, they noticed the electricity had returned. They also saw the town further down the hill was lit up. Text messages began flooding their phones the nearer they got to the house. James took out his phone and noticed he was finally getting a signal. Defeated, they marched into the house silently. Alister searched the kitchen cabinets until he found a bottle of bourbon. Ravi, James, and Heidi followed him into the kitchen, tears still wet on their faces. Alister lined up four glasses and poured them drinks. His hand shook uncontrollably as he picked up his glass and gulped down the drink while sniffling.

"Tell me this isn't real. Tell me that didn't just happen. This is just a bad dream, right? Right?!" said James.

"I don't understand; we had a plan. What the hell happened out there?" asked Ravi.

"I fucked up. I was supposed to light the stake before I stabbed Krampus, but I choked when I saw the Yule Goat about to attack both of you," Alister replied.

"You fucked up? That's all you have to say to me? Raphael is dead because you fucked up," Ravi raged.

"Wow, don't even start that," said James.

"He's right. I slipped up, and it cost the lives of three people," Alister responded.

"Damn right, you fucked up. But that doesn't bring them back, now does it! Dammit!" Ravi growled as he threw the glass at the wall.

"Ravi, that's enough!" James repeated.

"Let him be. He has every right to feel upset about this. He's right; I was too concerned about the lives of you and him that I got distracted out there, and I got Uncle Raph killed," Alister remarked.

"What do you mean our lives? You had a plan; this was your plan! How could you, of all people, get distracted!?" Ravi questioned.

"This was not my plan! I wanted to give my life to spare you and James," Alister shot back.

"Even if you did, it wouldn't have brought back my father," Ravi replied.

"This is because your father wouldn't let me. He's a hypocrite! He made me promise to not trade my life for yours, but he went and tried to do it anyway. He knew it wouldn't have worked if he had done it. He should have let me go out there from the jump," Alister retorted.

"What the hell are you talking about?" asked Ravi.

"Your dad didn't tell you the whole truth. Seeing the death omen, the Yule Goat, meant you needed to present it with a gift when it came on Christmas eve. It came for a life; if you didn't offer one to it, it would have killed you both, and we couldn't lift a finger to stop it," Alister answered.

"What?" said James.

"I was willing to be the sacrifice to keep you two

safe. I would have done anything for you, but he wouldn't let me. Then he turned around, offered himself, hoping it might work, and got himself killed. If he had let me just give up my worthless ass life, all of them would have still been here," Alister stated miserably.

"Alister...," James began.

"This is all your fault," Ravi snapped.

"Ravi—"Adelheid chastised.

Alister walked around the table and put down his glass. "How dare you!" said Alister.

"If you had stuck to either of the plans, my dad would still be here. Benji and Shay would still be here," Ravi stated.

Alister punched Ravi in the face. Ravi stumbled back and held his face. "You were the one who showed this place to me. You were the one who held me back when I tried to hand over myself and protect everyone. I was only looking out for my family. I would give anything to undo what happened here tonight. How dare you stand there and blame me for this! I know I messed up, but we wouldn't have been here if not for Heidi calling your dad. You would have never seen this place, and I never would have gotten it. So, get the fuck off your high horse.

"I am not the only one here. We all had a part to play in what happened here tonight. I did my best, just like everyone else, just like your dad. Uncle Raph made the same call I did. He promised to keep us all safe, and he died trying, and I wish I did, too," said Alister.

"I wish you did, too," Ravi agreed.

"You don't mean that," James exclaimed.

"Don't say that to me. Don't you dare say that to me! We're family," said Alister with tears in his eyes.

"Screw you… My family died trying to save me tonight," said Ravi as he walked away and went upstairs. Adelheid, stunned by his words, followed behind him.

Alister leaned over the table, shaking at the shoulders, his tears dripping onto the wooden countertop.

James was speechless. He had never seen Ravi act like this. Alister broke down and threw everything off the table.

"Alister…," James mumbled.

"James—," Alister replied.

"What are we going to tell everyone?" James asked.

Alister stayed silent for a bit.

"Alister?" James said.

"Nobody can know what really went down here. Uncle Raph tried to protect us from this. He would want us to do the same," Alister responded.

Ravi leaned over the balcony upstairs and looked down at them. "We'll tell them that my dad came and took them to see the Christmas celebrations in town. The three of us went on a hike in the mountain like we usually do when we are with him. When we returned, he was lying dead outside, the kids were missing, and Alyssa was alive but comatose. At least that way, they won't blame you for this mess," Ravi stated.

Alister and James looked up to Ravi. "I owe you this much. But after this, I don't think we can go back to being what we used to be. I trusted you, and you let me down. I get that you tried your best, but that will not bring back my dad. I'm sorry, Alister, but I can't let this go," Ravi declared before he walked off and closed the door to the room behind him.

"Fair enough," Alister whispered.

"Are you going to be ok?" asked James.

"No," said Alister.

"Come back home. We would need you now more than ever," James exclaimed.

"No, that's not what I meant. Alyssa still hasn't woken up. Krampus is still out there, so it really does make you wonder what else is out there in the dark," Alister remarked.

"You want to continue Uncle Raph's family legacy?" said James.

"It's personal now. I won't rest until I know it's dead. I'm going to hunt this creature down if it's the last thing I do," Alister declared.

"Not alone, you're not," James replied.

"James, you saw what happened here tonight," said Alister.

"Yeah, I did. Just imagine what would have happened if I was out there with you; we might have saved everyone!" James exclaimed.

"Or we could have both died," Alister responded.

"True, but I would rather die by your side than live without you, and I'm not asking," James stated as he extended his fist to Alister.

Alister chuckled and looked at him. "Alister and James, huh?" he said.

"Alister and James," James smirked, closing his hand. Their knuckles met as he thrusted his fist lightly to meet Alister's.

Alister's phone vibrated. He curiously took out his phone from his jacket pocket, and a voicemail appeared on the screen. Alister opened it and put the phone on loudspeaker. Raphael's voice echoed through the kitchen. "I'm about to do something stupid, but just in case, here goes. I didn't want to do this. I did everything to keep this away from you boys, but you show great potential, Alister. You might be better than I ever was. You remind me of my great-grandfather, Brij. If we survive this, come visit me when you return home. I will teach you everything I know. Krampus was one of the worst evils that roamed the earth, but it's not the only one. Every scary story has an origin in truth; the things that are really out there, they will come for you. So, you'll need to know how to protect your family like I have been doing all these years.

My library is yours to explore. Everything I learned about, every evil thing out there, is on those

pages. Commit them to memory when you can...."
They heard the sound of a door closing, and then
Raphael said, 'Son?' followed by Alister saying, 'We
need to talk.'" Alister quickly realized when this had
taken place.

"See, this is what he wanted. You were already
honoring his legacy. This just proves you were on the
right path," James exclaimed.

"I guess we were," Alister replied.

"By the way, do you remember the incantation he
was doing to cleanse the bullets and stakes? He said
that regular weapons won't work on these creatures.
So, that seems like something we would need to know
if we are going to hunt these creatures," James added.

"I don't know all the words to it, but I'm sure I
can find it online. I remembered how it started,
'Exorcizamus te.'"

AND THUS BEGAN THE TALE OF ALISTER
AND JAMES